P9-DCL-928

OVER THE MOON

Let Love In

Written by **Colin Hosten & Sia Dey**

Illustrated by **Yujia Wang & Brittany Myers**

HARPER

An Imprint of HarperCollinsPublishers

Over the Moon © 2020 Netflix and Pearl Studio.
Used with permission.

All rights reserved. Manufactured in Italy.
No part of this book may be used or reproduced
in any manner whatsoever without written permission
except in the case of brief quotations embodied in critical
articles and reviews. For information address
HarperCollins Children's Books, a division of HarperCollins
Publishers, 195 Broadway, New York, NY 10007.

www.harpercollinschildrens.com

Library of Congress Control Number: 2020937804

ISBN: 978-0-06-300241-8

20 21 22 23 24   RTLO   10 9 8 7 6 5 4 3 2 1
❖
First Edition

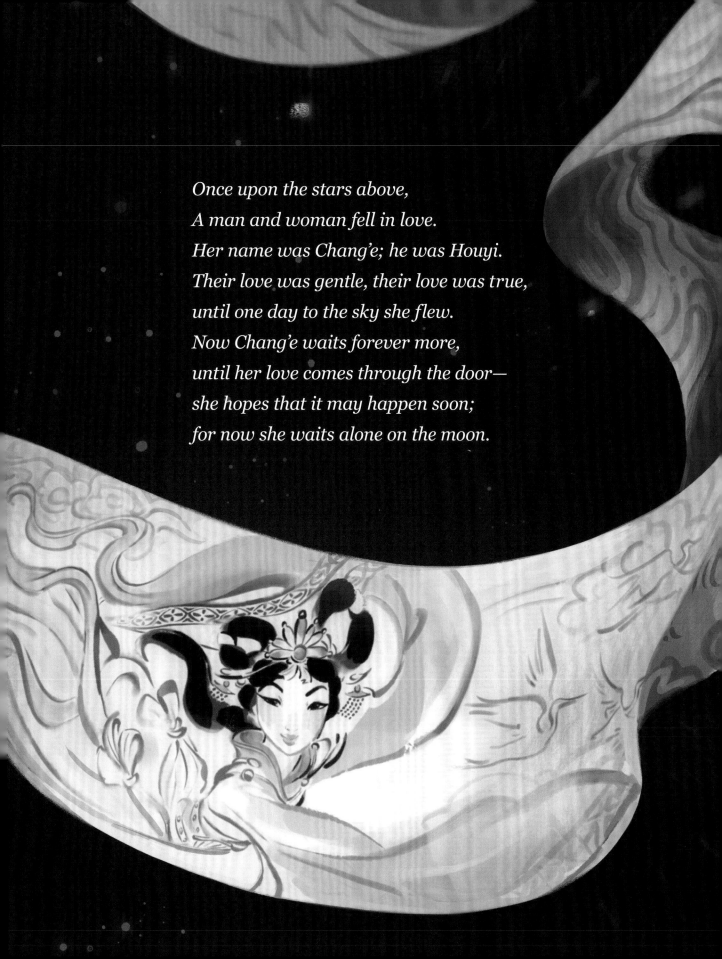

Once upon the stars above,
A man and woman fell in love.
Her name was Chang'e; he was Houyi.
Their love was gentle, their love was true,
until one day to the sky she flew.
Now Chang'e waits forever more,
until her love comes through the door—
she hopes that it may happen soon;
for now she waits alone on the moon.

Fei Fei loved when mother told her
the story of Chang'e, the moon goddess.
It always made the little girl happy.
As her mother would say . . .

Cherish life, Fei Fei.
Love those around you,
each and every day.

Keep filling our mooncakes with magic.
Remember to always do your best.
Cherish life, stay true, and always know,
I . . . love . . . you. . . .

Sometimes, we have to say goodbye
to the ones we cherish most in life

As days turned to years, the family began to heal. And though they had each other, it was time to meet new people. What Fei Fei didn't want was a *new* family. Fei Fei already had Bungee the rabbit and her father, Baba.

Fei Fei looked to the stars
and thought of the moon goddess.
If only Fei Fei could prove Chang'e was real,
it would remind Baba of mother's love.

Oh, Chang'e, what can I do?
How can I prove your story true?

That's it, Fei Fei thought. I'll build a rocket ship.

That's the answer, Chang'e.
I hope to see you soon!

We're on our way, in my rocket to the moon!

This will not come easy,
Fei Fei thought.

We might crash,

we might fall,

but we must never give up.

Together, they found an extraordinary place,
A magical world full of wondrous light.

Soon, Fei Fei found the moon goddess, Chang'e. . . .

She was spectacular! Extraordinary! *Ultraluminary!* But Fei Fei quickly learned not everything was as it seemed.

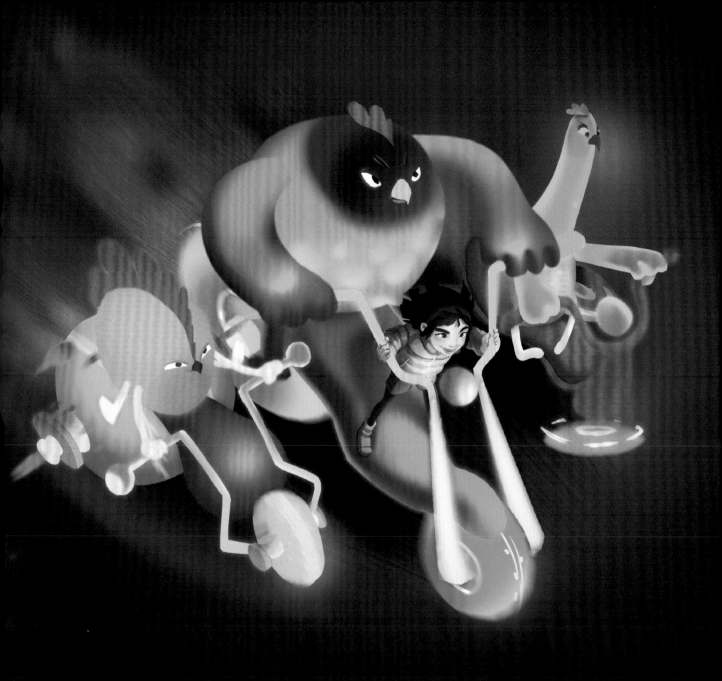

Chang'e promised Fei Fei answers to her
questions, but first, a quest!

The brave girl accepted. Now Fei Fei must
journey across the moon to find the moon
goddess a special gift.

Fei Fei searched far and wide. But she could not find the gift. She *did* find biker chicks, moon frogs, and a new friend named Gobi.

Gobi loved to *glow* and encouraged Fei Fei to never give up, but to *grow*.

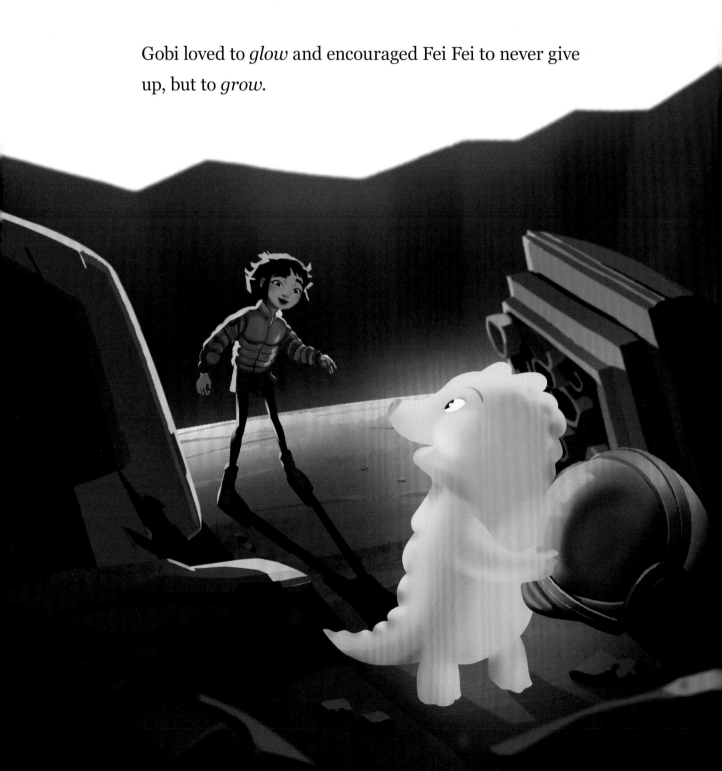

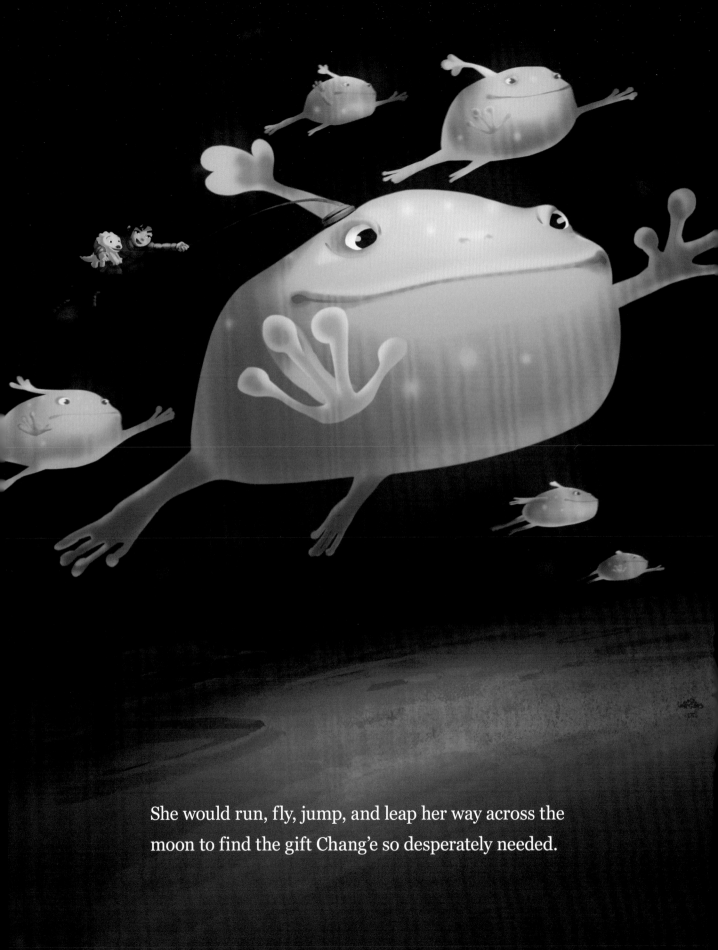

She would run, fly, jump, and leap her way across the
moon to find the gift Chang'e so desperately needed.

And just when she thought she had *found* the gift,
Fei Fei had *lost* it, whatever "it" was.
The little girl became sad.

Very, very sad.

The moon goddess reminded Fei Fei that
there were those who still *loved*.
All we had to do was let *them* in.

Let *love* in.

And so she did.

Fei Fei learned there are those who love us
willing to break through anything to reach us.

Fei Fei needed to let love through,
to embrace what was always there.

And so she did.

Fei Fei finally realized that *love* was the gift . . .

. . . and *love* was all *around* her and always *had* been.

We may say goodbye to the ones we love.

We may say goodbye to old friends who were always there.

What we realize is that we are never alone.
And with that, Fei Fei and her new brother
decided to head home.

*It was time to release the past,
to move ahead, to bloom at last.*

To *glow*.

To *grow*.

If you can give love, if you can let love through,
you'll find your family waiting there for you.

PROPERTY OF BLUFF
SCHOOL
(Fish Tank)

P9-DGV-961

LANDED

Milly Lee

Pictures by Yangsook Choi

Frances Foster Books Farrar, Straus and Giroux / New York

For Sun Chor's great-grandchildren: Christopher, Nicholas, Michela, Jonathan, Emi, and Matthew   —M.L.

To my father   —Y.C.

Text copyright © 2006 by Milly Lee
Pictures copyright © 2006 by Yangsook Choi
All rights reserved
Color separations by Chroma Graphics PTE Ltd.
Printed in China by RR Donnelley Asia Printing Solutions Ltd.,
Dongguan City, Guangdong Province
Designed by Nancy Goldenberg
First edition, 2006
10

mackids.com

Library of Congress Cataloging-in-Publication Data
Lee, Milly.
    Landed / Milly Lee ; pictures by Yangsook Choi.— 1st ed.
        p.   cm.
    Summary: After leaving his home in southeastern China, twelve-year-old Sun is held and
interrogated on Angel Island before being allowed to join his merchant father in San Francisco.
Includes historical notes.
    ISBN: 978-0-374-34314-9
    1. Chinese Americans—Juvenile fiction.   [1. Chinese Americans—Fiction.
2. Immigrants—Fiction.   3. China—History—20th century—Fiction.   4. Angel Island
(Calif.)—History—20th century—Fiction.   5. San Francisco (Calif.)—History—20th
century—Fiction.]   I. Choi, Yangsook, ill.   II. Title.

PZ7.L51433Lan 2006
[E]—dc22

                                                                                    2004047216

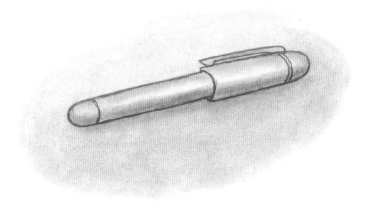

On his twelfth birthday, Sun's parents gave him an American fountain pen. At dinner, Father served him the choicest piece of the fish, and his mother looked sad.

The following morning, Sun was summoned to his father's study. Something important is going to happen, Sun thought.

Sun bowed as he greeted his father—"Good morning, BaBa"—and then his tutor—"Good morning, Mr. Chan."

"Our village is small," began Father, "so we must go where there are more opportunities. Now that you are twelve years old, I will take you with me to America."

Sun was pleased, but he wasn't completely surprised. His father was a merchant who traveled to America every few years. His store in San Francisco, Suen Yuen Hing, imported food from China to sell and ship to Chinese stores and restaurants throughout America.

Sun knew that his three older brothers had gone to America soon after they turned twelve. Ming, who was only two years older, was the brother he missed the most. Doh and Duc had left home a long time ago.

"Please, BaBa, when will we leave?" implored Sun.

"Soon," his father answered, "but first you must be coached by Mr. Chan so that you can answer all the questions that will be asked of you. Your brothers and I gave the American officials information about our family, our home, and our village when we entered the country. You will be interrogated to prove you are my true son."

Father looked serious. "One wrong answer, and you might be sent back to China."

"I will study hard, BaBa, I promise. I will learn everything I must know," replied Sun.

Mr. Chan told Sun that the best way to remember something was to find the answers yourself. "If you are going to be asked about your house, you must know all the details. You will need to know how many windows there are, the directions the doors face, what each room is used for, and where the kitchen stove is placed. Make a plan of the house showing everything," instructed Mr. Chan.

Sun was surprised at the number of windows; he had never counted them before. He worked all day to put on paper everything he observed about the house.

The next day, Mr. Chan told Sun to make a chart showing every member of the Lee family. Sun arranged the names according to their generation and their place in the family. He started with his paternal grandparents, followed by his parents and the aunts and uncles; then his brothers and sisters and himself, and all the cousins.

Besides the surname, each generation in the family shared a common name; Chor was the name Sun and his siblings and cousins shared. Sun's full name was Lee Sun Chor.

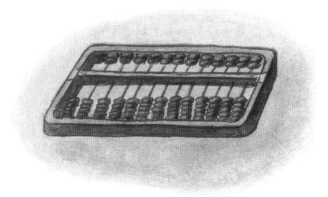

In the days that followed, Sun drew maps of everything in the village: the farms, the school, and the cemetery where family members were buried. He showed the wells, bridges, streams, and roads. Mr. Chan told him to indicate the compass points—East, South, West, and North*—but Sun always had trouble figuring directions.

"Remember," Mr. Chan explained, "the sun rises in the east. From that you can figure out south, west, and north no matter where you are." Sun wished his brother Ming, who always kept a compass in his pocket, were there to help him.

"What is the distance between your house and the school?" asked Mr. Chan.

Sun thought. "I will count my steps to the school," he said. But when he started to count, he found that he lost track too easily. He decided to make a mark for each 10 steps he took. He walked and made 176 marks, or 1,760 steps.

"You must figure the distance more precisely," said Mr. Chan.

So Sun measured his stride as well. Then he used his abacus to calculate the distance. He came up with an answer of two *li* (about two thirds of a mile).

"The distance between my house and the school is two *li*," answered Sun.

Mr. Chan was pleased that Sun had found a way to measure the distance. He referred to the coaching book Sun's father had prepared for them with questions to ask. He taught Sun how to use his own maps, house plans, and charts to remember the answers.

*The Chinese compass, called "water south needle," was invented in the fourth century in China. The Chinese use "East, South, West, North" in that order when they refer to direction.

Everyone in the small village knew Sun was going to America. A neighbor asked Sun if he would return with large pieces of gold from Gum Saan, Gold Mountain, which was what people called America.

Sun was measured for Western clothes and fitted with new leather shoes. His mother sewed a small hidden pocket on the inside of his vest.

Sun visited the graves of his ancestors to bid them farewell. He lit ceremonial candles and incense, offered food, and poured wine on their graves. Then he bowed three times and asked them to watch over him in America.

The big day arrived. After breakfast, the entire family, including the servants and Mr. Chan, lined up in front of the house to bid farewell to Sun and his father. Two sedan chairs and porters had been hired to take them and their luggage to the train station in Canton for the six-hour trip to Hong Kong.

In Hong Kong, Father arranged for pedicabs to take them to the ship. The ride across the noisy city was bumpy and exciting. They made their way through crowds of rickshaws, carts, animals, and people on foot. When they reached the dock, they saw the SS *President Taft*.

Sun had never imagined the ship would be so large. As they moved up the gangplank, Sun looked back to see the jostling crowd of well-dressed Caucasian men and women, South Asian women in colorful saris and men in turbans, and well-to-do Chinese people behind them. Many more of their countrymen, struggling with large bundles of clothing and food, pushed their way onto a lower deck.

Sun and his father found their stateroom. Four bunk beds, a small corner sink, a chest of drawers, and a chair took up most of the space. Father said it would be best to use the bottom bunks for sleeping and the top bunks for their suitcases.

He took Sun to find the shared bathrooms. Then they went up on deck, where passengers crowded at the rail, waving and tossing colorful streamers to people below. A loud blast from the ship's whistle signaled their departure. The gangplanks were raised, and the ship slowly left the dock. Sun and his father watched until the city had faded away and open sea surrounded them.

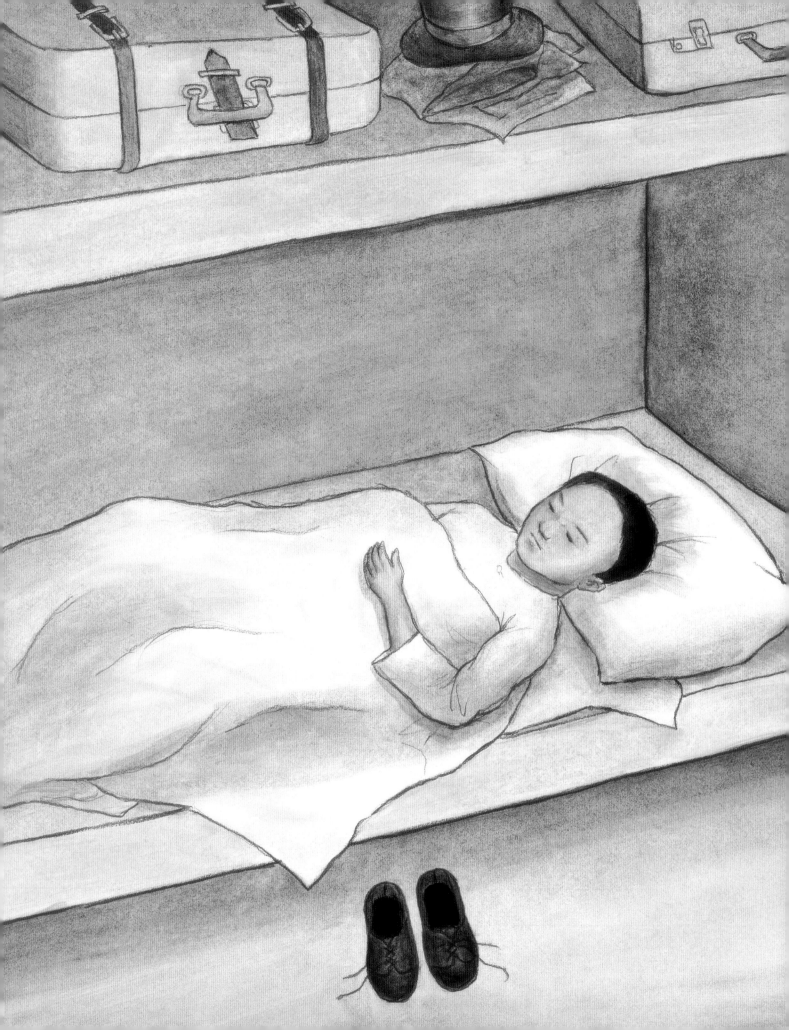

Their early departure from home and the excitement of the day made Sun very tired, but he was unable to sleep. He thought about the journey to America; he was afraid that he might not do well in the interrogations. What if he forgot all that he had learned? He tried to remember how far it was from his home to his school—and he couldn't. He started counting the windows in his house. What if he failed? The gentle movement of the ship lulled him to sleep despite his many worries.

Chimes sounded, waking Sun. "That is the call for breakfast," said Father, who was already up and dressed. Sun was hungry; he had been too excited to eat much at dinner the night before.

There were mostly businessmen, with some students and just a few families, at the early seating in their second-class dining room. Sun and his father were assigned to table number 8, with a South Asian family en route to England. After a brief introduction in English by the two fathers, they all ate with little conversation. Mr. Chan had taught Sun how to use forks, spoons, and knives, so he was comfortable eating Western style.

Of all the strange new foods Sun tasted during the twenty-two days on board the SS *President Taft*, his favorites were pineapple juice, fried potatoes, beef steaks, bacon, and cookies. He did not like milk.

After breakfast, they walked around the deck and Father asked questions from Sun's coaching book. Sun had never spent so much time with his father. He enjoyed having his attention, although he soon grew tired of the testing.

"BaBa, please tell me about America," implored Sun. "I want to know where we will live and what I will do there. Will I be with my brothers? Will I go to school?"

"Too many questions, my son," Father said, laughing, "but I will try to answer them. You will go to school with your brothers, and you will also work at the store. Our living space is in back of the store."

Sun asked, "Will I return home someday?"

Father replied, "You will return home to marry, but first you must learn English and many things about America."

"BaBa, are there really gold nuggets on the streets of Gum Saan for anyone to pick up?" asked Sun.

"No, that's a myth. We all work hard in Gum Saan," said Father. "But with hard work there are many ways to succeed in America."

When he wasn't with his father, Sun explored the ship on his own. He could go wherever he wanted except to the top, first-class deck. Father told him the lower decks were where most of their countrymen stayed.

Sun's favorite place was the library. There were many books and magazines with pictures that he could look at even if he couldn't read the English words. Father showed him on a globe where they lived in Kow Kong village, in Guangdong Province in southeast China—and where San Francisco was in America. It was a long way across the Pacific Ocean.

On the last night of the voyage, Father gave Sun his identification card. "Keep this in a safe place," he said. "I will disembark before you because I am a returning merchant. You will go to Angel Island to be interviewed and questioned without me. I do not know how long you will be held there, but I will be informed when you have passed your tests. I will meet you when you come ashore."

Sun put the identification card in the hidden inside pocket that his mother had sewn to his vest. Then Father tore up the pages of the coaching book and threw them overboard. As the papers disappeared in the sea, Sun thought: Now I have only my memory to get me to America.

Sun and his father were up early the next morning. They saw the northern coast of California just before they entered San Francisco Bay. When the ship docked, American officials came aboard to process the passengers. The first group to be called were tourists coming to San Francisco for the Panama Pacific International Exposition.

When returning travelers were called, Father touched Sun lightly on his shoulder, and left.

"Goodbye, BaBa," said Sun bravely. He felt very alone and frightened as he watched his father leave.

A loud announcement in Cantonese directed passengers arriving in America for the first time to assemble in the main lounge. Sun picked up his suitcase and moved toward the meeting place. There he saw many more of his countrymen, some women and children, too. Almost everybody looked as scared as Sun felt. They were told to have their identification cards ready to show before boarding the motor launch that would take them to Angel Island.

It was a cold, gray day, and the ride was bumpy as the launch headed through the fog for the island in the middle of San Francisco Bay. American guards in green uniforms met the arriving boat. Sun climbed the ladder to the pier and followed the others to a two-story wooden building. After the women and younger children were led away to separate quarters, the men and boys were told to strip to the waist and form a line.

Sun was frightened and embarrassed. He had never undressed in public. He did as he was told, but avoided looking at anyone.

American doctors in white coats listened to his chest, looked down his throat, and checked his scalp for lice. Sun's face flushed with humiliation. He felt shamed even though he was told that he had passed the examination and was allowed to dress again. He was led up a flight of stairs to a large dormitory filled with rows and rows of bunk beds, stacked three high. The lower bunks had been claimed by immigrants already there. Sun found a top bunk near a window. The windows had bars. The door was locked behind them. Angel Island was like a prison.

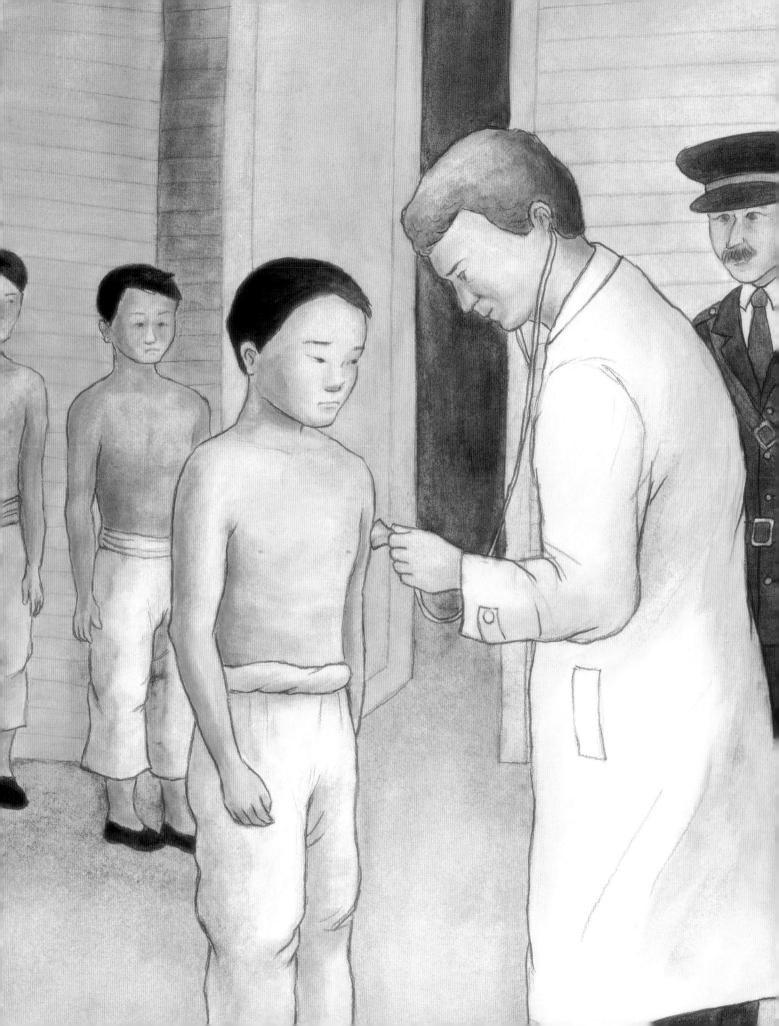

A boy a little older than Sun came over to introduce himself. "I am Hop Jeong from Sun Cheun village. I have been here for five weeks." Hop waved a hand to encourage another boy to come over.

Five weeks—that's a long time, thought Sun.

"I am Puy Gong from Cha Yuen village. I have been here for twenty weeks. I was denied entry, but my case is being appealed. They tell me it can take as much as a year to win an appeal."

A year! How long will I be here? wondered Sun. "I am Sun Chor from Kow Kong village," he said.

The sound of a key in the door alerted everyone that it was time for lunch. They crowded into the aisle, and rushed out when the door opened. It was not because they were so hungry but because they wanted to leave the room.

The dining room was big enough for a hundred people to eat at one time. There were spoons, bowls, and chopsticks at each table. A bowl of vegetables and meat came with a larger bowl of rice. The three boys quickly filled their bowls. Hop showed Sun where to sit to get the food first. Sometimes there wasn't enough to go around, so it was best to be among the first to help themselves to the food.

After lunch, everybody was allowed to go out to the fenced yard for some fresh air. Hop looked around to make sure no one was listening before quietly asking, "Are you a paper son?"

"What is a paper son?" asked Sun.

"You don't know?"

"No."

Hop explained to Sun that some families sent boys who claimed to be sons of returning merchants and U.S. citizens so they could be admitted into the country. He said these boys used coaching books to learn all they could about their paper families. It was the only way they could come to America.

"Here on Angel Island," he told Sun, "the Immigration officers try hard to catch these boys in errors and deport them. I am a paper son," confided Hop softly.

"I, too, am a paper son," whispered Puy Gong. "The Immigration officer suspects I am not who I claim to be, so my family has paid an attorney to appeal my case."

"I am a true son," said Sun. "My father is a merchant, but I studied my coaching book so I would be able to remember all the details of my family and home. My father says I should not have any trouble. I'll be all right unless they ask me about direction."

Long days of waiting with little to do but eat and sleep stretched in front of them. When would they be questioned? The boys spent part of every day drilling themselves on the questions and answers they had memorized. Some of the immigrants played Chinese dominoes or cards to pass the time.

Carved into the walls of their dormitory room were poems written by those who had been there before them. Some of the poems were sad and bitter. Sun read them aloud to the boys because neither one knew how to read. Puy Gong and Hop had learned their coaching books by listening and memorizing every question and answer.

One morning, Hop was called for questioning. Puy Gong and Sun watched quietly as Hop prepared himself by washing his face, combing his hair, and putting on a clean shirt.

Hop was gone for three hours. The two friends waited anxiously. When he returned he told the boys it was "not too bad." He had been asked many questions about his family and his village and could answer most except for questions about his uncles.

The following day, Hop was called again and was questioned for two more hours. He was asked many of the same questions as the day before.

"They wanted to see if you would answer the same way," said Puy Gong.

Hop was called for a third interrogation. The next day, he was told he would be "landed." He had passed and would be allowed to leave Angel Island to go ashore to Gum Saan.

Sun said goodbye to his friend; he asked Hop to try to see his father at his store, Suen Yuen Hing, on Grant Avenue to tell him Sun was fine.

Four weeks later, Sun's name was called. He had been dreading this moment, but he was glad the waiting and the suspense were ending. Now he had to do everything right so he would not shame his family. He put on his new Western clothes, hoping to make a good impression. He took the identification card from his hidden vest pocket.

"Good luck," murmured Puy Gong.

Sun was taken into a small room. Seated at a table were two American officials. A Chinese interpreter instructed Sun to sit in a chair facing the two men. An American woman, the recorder, was seated at a small table next to them.

After checking Sun's identification card, the men compared him to the picture and information they had about his age, height, and weight. The questions started: "What is your father's name? How many brothers and sisters do you have? What are their names?" Sun answered them easily.

Each time one of the American officials asked a question, the Chinese interpreter would translate it into Cantonese for Sun. The interpreter translated Sun's answers into English for the American officials. The woman recorded all the questions and answers. That took a long time.

"How many rooms are there in your house? How many windows? Where is the well?" Sun felt confident; he was glad Mr. Chan had him do the maps and floor plans of his house so that he could answer the questions.

"Which direction does your bedroom face?" Sun tried to think, but his mind was blank. "I don't know," he said. They asked again, but Sun could not answer. Besides, he was tired. The questions went on and on: "How many steps from your house to the nearest house? Who lives there? Which direction does the house face?"

Sun paused—which direction? His heart raced. He looked at the interpreter. "I don't know," he answered.

When the question was asked a second time, Sun looked down at the floor. He could not answer.

"You'll have to come back tomorrow," said the interpreter, as the officials signaled the end of the session.

That night, Sun lay awake in the dark room. He thought about the questions he could not answer. He pictured himself walking around his house and saw where the sun rose each morning: that would be east. He continued through the house, and out the door to the house closest to his, where the Fungs lived. Which direction did it face? He wished his brother Ming were there to help him.

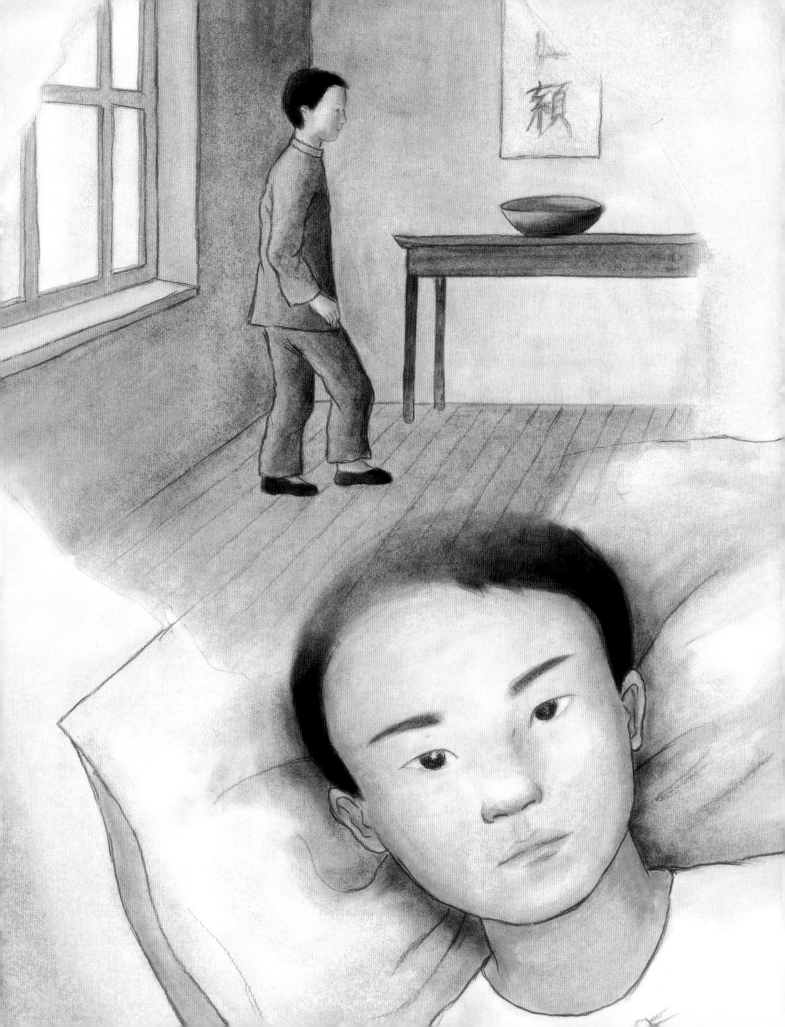

Sun was called again the next afternoon, and again he wore his Western clothes. And again he was asked about direction. He closed his eyes and tried imagining how he would walk through his house, out the door, and to the village. He moved his hands, one pointing east and the other in the direction of the village; still, he was confused. "I don't know," replied Sun.

"You will have to return again tomorrow," said the interpreter.

That night, at dinner, someone handed a box of cookies to Sun and said in a low voice, "This is from your father. There's something extra in the box for you. Take it out when you are alone."

"Thank you," said Sun.

Back in his bunk, Sun reached into the box and moved his hand around carefully. He felt something small and round and took it out . . . Ming's compass!

Sun held on to the compass all night.

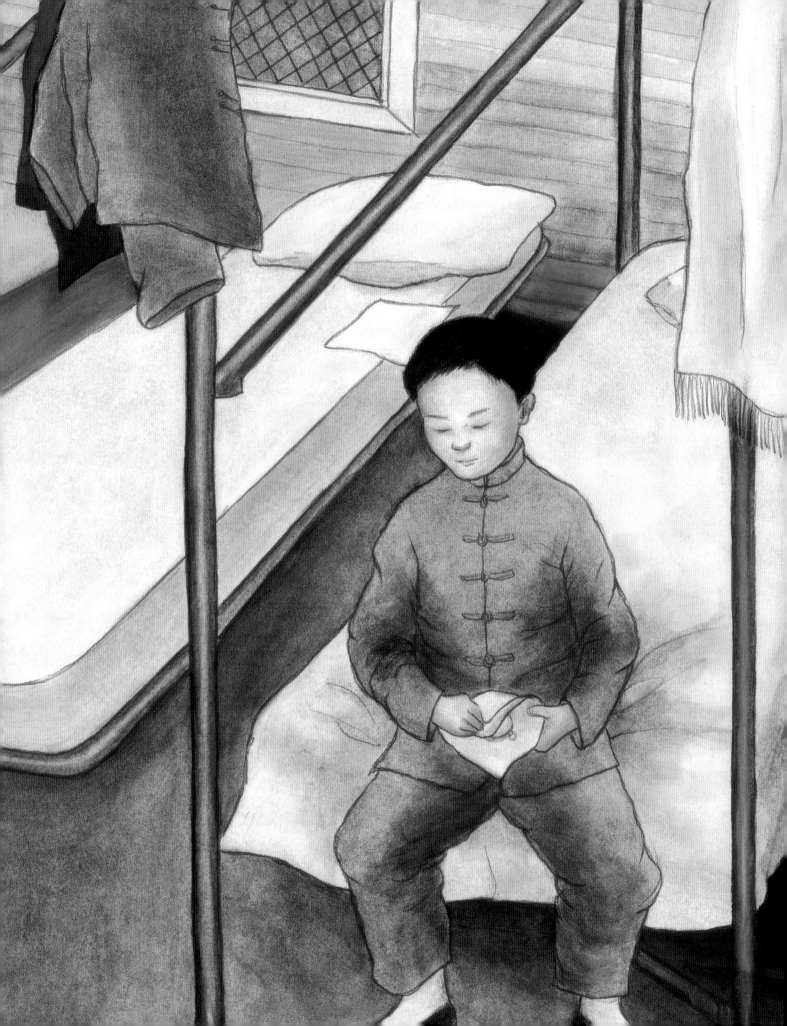

The next morning, before he returned to the interrogation room, Sun slipped the compass into his hidden pocket.

After a series of questions, Sun was asked what direction he traveled to go from home to school. He mentally went to the front door of his house, then looked in the direction of where the school would be. Reaching into his secret pocket, he took out Ming's compass. If the front door faced east, he thought, then the school was to the north.

He looked straight at the interpreter. "North," he answered.

"What does he have in his hand?" one of the officials asked brusquely. "Where did he get it? Let me see it." The interpreter told Sun to give him the compass.

"I use it to help me with direction," said Sun quietly as he handed it over.

The interpreter passed it to the officials, explaining, "It's just a compass."

They examined it carefully.

The two officials talked quietly with each other for a moment. Then they put the compass on the table and began filling out paperwork. The room grew quiet.

The interpreter turned to Sun. "They have decided that it is all right to use a compass. Since it would not help someone who didn't already know the information, they have concluded that you are telling the truth."

Sun slept better that night. He knew that he had answered the questions correctly. All he could do now was hold on to Ming's compass and hope for the best.

Early the next morning, the guard called out: "Lee Sun Chor, you are landed."

Sun quickly packed and was ready to leave. He said goodbye to Puy Gong and wished him luck with his case. He boarded the motor launch for the short ride to San Francisco. Halfway across the bay, the sun broke through the fog, revealing the city shining golden in the morning sun. Gum Saan!

As the launch drew up to the pier, Sun could see his father. He didn't know the three men with him until he recognized Ming and realized these three grown men were his brothers.

Sun could hardly wait for the launch to dock. With just a few steps up a ladder, then ten paces on the pier, Sun was reunited with his family. He had landed.

AUTHOR'S NOTE

The Chinese came to California in great numbers during the Gold Rush in the 1850s; in the 1860s they came to work on the transcontinental railroad. When cheap labor was no longer needed in the 1870s, the Chinese were blamed for the bad economic times and were attacked and driven out of many communities throughout the West. The Chinese Exclusion Act, enacted by Congress in 1882, barred the further immigration of Chinese laborers to the United States. European immigrants were permitted entry when they arrived at Ellis Island on the East Coast, while on the West Coast, immigration officers at Angel Island tried to keep the Chinese out. Only merchants, students, diplomats, and tourists were allowed entry. These laws were so effective that in 1887 only ten Chinese were admitted.

When official records were lost in the 1906 San Francisco earthquake and fire, the Chinese saw an opportunity to claim they were U.S. citizens and report a number of children born in China regardless of whether this was true or not. Chinese merchants were also known to report newborn children each time they returned from a visit to China. These claims created "immigration slots" by which a Chinese could later pose as a son of a U.S. citizen or merchant on paper, thus the term "paper son." Individual coaching books were prepared to ensure that the information these paper sons gave matched the information given by their alleged fathers. The paper sons memorized the questions and answers about their paper families and villages and destroyed their coaching books before arrival. True sons, like Sun, also studied from coaching books, to ensure they would pass the interrogations and not be deported. While food packages sent to detainees from Chinatown were allowed, they were first inspected by immigration authorities to make sure they didn't contain hidden coaching notes. The immigration officials detained the Chinese immigrants until satisfied the boys were who they claimed to be.

After he was landed, Sun attended school in San Francisco and worked in his father's store. He went back to China to be married and then returned to America to work. His wife and son arrived in 1939 on tourist visas. The Chinese Exclusion Act was repealed in 1943, and the Chinese were finally granted the right to become naturalized U.S. citizens. As a result, Sun became a U.S. citizen after World War II, as did his wife and son.

This story, told to me by my father-in-law, Lee Sun Chor, is just one of many stories of the Angel Island experience yet to be told. I am grateful to Hop Jeong, who shared his story and copies of interrogation transcripts with me. Historian Dr. Judy Yung and Angel Island Immigration Station Foundation's Erika Gee shared their expertise. For more information, visit the Angel Island Immigration Station Foundation Web site at www.aiisf.org/.